Spring Break
with
Paddy O'Rourke
Book II

to   Daniel

Patti B. Pruitt

Spring Break
with
Paddy O'Rourke
Book II

by

Patti B. Pruitt

DORRANCE PUBLISHING CO., INC.
PITTSBURGH, PENNSYLVANIA 15222

ISBN: 978-1-4349-0163-7
Library of Congress Control Number: 2008941590

Printed in the United States of America

First Printing

For information or to order additional books, please contact:
Dorrance Publishing Co., Inc.
701 Smithfield Street
Pittsburgh, Pennsylvania 15222
U.S.A.
1-800-788-7654
www.dorrancebookstore.com

Dedication

Book two, Spring Break with Paddy O'Rourke, is also dedicated to my grandfather, Edward Jason McLaughlin. His letters and stories of Paddy O'Rourke are forever in my heart and on my mind as I sit at his old roll-top desk and write.

Special thanks to my husband and daughters for all the spring breaks that we enjoyed. Those memories will be cherished forever.

Last, thanks to my grandchildren, who never get tired of my stories of Paddy O'Rourke. They are my biggest fans, and I love them with all my heart.

Reader's Note

Because all of the leprechauns and Irish characters in this book speak with an Irish accent, I spelled some of their words and phrases as they are pronounced in Ireland. I hope this does not cause too much confusion for children.

Chapter One

I was right. My life would never be the same again. It had been several months since Grampa Mac had introduced me to my very own little leprechaun named Paddy O'Rourke, and I was still amazed. This past Christmas and ski trip had been very exciting. I never knew if the silly things happening to me were the doings of my new little friend Paddy or his ornery uncle Huey O'Rourke. I was pretty sure Paddy's girlfriend, Lily, was not the culprit. She had a cute smile and a way of making Paddy behave that I will never understand.

Grampa Mac and I had had many long talks since Christmas, and I was getting quite comfortable when Paddy would suddenly show up. Being a master of mischief, Paddy would suddenly make a surprise appearance, so it was not unusual for me to look in the mirror after brushing my teeth and see Paddy sitting on my shoulder. Since he was only four inches tall and weighed mere ounces, I never felt him sitting on my shoulder or on top of my head and would jump when I saw him. I have also grown accustomed to the way Paddy contacts me if he wants to talk to me seriously—the pipe.

I sometimes will smell the wonderful scent of his tiny little pipe, and I know to go to a private place where we can talk alone. That has only happened a few times because it is much more fun for Paddy or Huey to scare the pants off me by sneaking up on me.

Fun for them, that is.

I may never get used to the fact that people laugh when I suddenly jump up off my chair when I sit on a pinecone. Or when my shoes suddenly become untied and I fall on my face. Or when I come home from school and my hair is standing straight up in a style that I myself am quite sure I did not do that morning.

Then there was the time my teacher smiled at me when she thought I had drawn hearts on my homework paper. Now hearts, you understand, are reserved only for moms and grammas when you are a kid, so I am once again positive I did not draw them.

I got an A on that report, so my mom did not have to sign it; therefore it went directly into the trash. Sometimes I just have to take matters into my own hands.

"Jason," my mom called. "Where are you?"

"I am in my room," I yelled back. I was laying on the floor in front of my window letting the sunlight warm me.

"Well, come down and help me in the garage please," she said.

Rats. The sun felt pretty good after a cold game of football outside. It was still March, and I loved playing outside. I was just laying there thinking about our trip to Destin in a few weeks. My mom had rented a condo right on the beach, and we were all excited about the trip and our new swimsuits and towels.

I use the term *excited* loosely, since my sisters—Shannon, six, and Amy, four—were much more enthused than I was. Jennifer was only two and did not mind running around naked, so all items of clothing were optional for her. Just so my swim trunks have a zippered inside pocket to keep change for the Coke and candy machines is all I care about. I had been saving my money from yard work jobs in the neighborhood. I had become quite the handyman with the blower and rake. I was also saving for my own lawnmower so I could make more money this summer. And I had lots of plans for that extra money.

I went to the garage and helped my mom move boxes around so we could stack the new floats and noodles and cooler we had bought for the trip. Everything was going as planned. I did not like the fact that my mom's sister had booked a place in the same city as us, because that meant that my bratty cousins, Greg and David, would once again be within a hundred miles of me.

My aunt Nancy had chosen a condo on the other side of Destin, and my mom and dad would not make us go over and visit them. I thought of all the fun we would have since my friends Jack, Rob, Kelly, Patrick, and Bobby had also booked a condo in our complex. Now I would not have to play with my sisters. I could do the more manly things, like Frisbee, volleyball, surfing, and snorkeling. I thought about all these things as I put up the items on the shelves.

"Mom," I asked. "how long will it take to get to Destin?"

"About six hours," she replied.

I looked up at my mom, and she had an enormous bird feather sticking out of her hair. I burst out laughing, and she looked at me like I was crazy.

"What is so funny?" she asked.

"You have a huge feather sticking up on your head," I replied.

"Where did that come from?" she asked. She looked around, then handed it to me.

I picked up some more things and handed them to her, then I headed back up to my room.

"Paddy, did you put that feather in Mom's hair?" I asked my empty room.

"Sure and begorra, 'twas me, laddie," replied the little man who was suddenly sitting on my bedpost. "Just thought ye may need a wee laugh."

"Well, she did look pretty funny, and it did make me laugh," I told him. "Where have you been Paddy? I have not seen you in a few weeks."

"Ah, 'twas the time of me life, laddie. Lily and I were at the St. Patrick's Day Leprechaun Playoffs in Ireland. Me uncle Huey and I ended up being the last two contestants, and 'twas nearly a fight to go down in the record books. For nearly three hundred years we have been neck and neck to the finish, but I took the lead this year and never let it go. 'Twas one of me finer moments, laddie."

"'Twas because ye cheated," said a voice from the other bedpost.

Uncle Huey appeared and had his usual ornery look on his face. He was shaking his hat in anger. Suddenly I had two little leprechauns sitting on my bedposts. One was happy and smiling, and one was not.

"Did not cheat once," said Paddy.

"Did too. Ye had yer pretty little girlfriend, Lily, around every corner with a piece of me favorite green chocolate cake and a bottle of me favorite green chocolate milk to go with it."

"Well, ye did not have to stop and eat every piece of cake and drink every ounce of milk," chuckled Paddy. "I meself had the willpower to resist."

"That's because yer favorite apple pie and green ice cream was not being offered to ye at every turn."

"Ye know full well, ye scoundrel," growled Huey. "And to think sweet little Lily would partake in such degrading assaults on me leprachaunal lust for cake and milk hurts me soul."

"Ah, hurts ye as much as ye hurt me last year when ye kept making me pants fall down just as I neared the finish lines so you could take the lead?"

I started laughing as I listened to the two of them bickering. I could just picture what they were saying.

"What kind of races were you running?" I asked.

"Oh, just the usual, cliff climbing, one-legged potato sack race, grasshopper riding rodeo, dolphin racing, balloon floating, tricycle trotting, band aid pull, slingshot derby, boomerang ducking, tree sawing, cricket jumping, domino falling, card house building, bubble blowing, potato shooting, and—me personal favorite—mole tipping."

"You both did all that?" I asked. "How do you tip a mole?"

"'Tis the truth, sure and begorra," said Paddy. "And we did all that in one week. Course, it took us two weeks to get into shape, but the best leprechaun won the gold medal."

"'Twas only because ye tricked me," yelled Huey as he jumped up and down on the bedpost. "And ye may as well admit it, ye little twerp," he added.

"Admit what? That ye had over two hundred years of practice on me? Are ye so much older than me that ye don't remember?"

With that comment Uncle Huey's face grew red, his mouth gripped his little pipe, and his whole body shook with fury. He waved his pointed little hat furiously, lost his balance, and fell onto my bed.

Paddy burst out laughing and said, "With balance like that, I am surprised ye came in second to yers truly."

And with that, he bowed to Uncle Huey and broke into more fits of laughter. Soon we all three were laughing, and Huey seemed to forget his anger and began smoothing out his hat. As everyone knows, it is not good luck nor appropriate for a leprechaun's hat to be wrinkled.

Chapter Two

It was a warm sunny day as our car pulled into the condo. Destin had to be the coolest place I had ever seen. Everywhere we looked were putt-putt golf courses, go-carts, water bumper boats, and even bungee jumping. It was a good bet that my eight-year-old body would not be experiencing the bungee thrill though. My mom was on the cautious side of parenting. I once again felt the money in my pocket. It was practically burning a hole in my pants.

I had been saving my money from last summer and from my winter chores so that I could have a really good spring break. All winter I had blown and raked leaves for neighbors and even walked the big dogs of old Miss Maude. She sometimes paid me with cookies and milk and sometimes with hugs, but mostly with shiny silver dollars which I heard she collected. My mom said they are very old, and so she swaps them out with dollar bills and puts them away somewhere we kids are not supposed to look.

"Okay guys," my dad said. "Everybody grab a bag, stay out of the way of cars, and follow me to the condo."

He had brought back a rolling luggage cart to put all of our suitcases on, and we carried the ones that would not fit.

"As soon as we get these upstairs, Dad will take you down to the pool while I begin unpacking," my mom said.

After Dad carefully and masterfully stacked the luggage cart, we were ready to roll. *Oops!*

Every suitcase shifted and fell off. Dad reloaded, much to our groans since he took much longer this time.

And soon we were off again.

Oops!

Yes indeed, they all came tumbling down once again. Everybody around was laughing really hard. Everybody except Mom and Dad that is.

This time Dad stacked with such painstaking slowness that we were about to explode, but it held and soon we were in the elevator.

And for reason we were stopping on every floor. Funny how things like that happen to me lately. I looked around but saw nobody suspicious sitting there laughing at us.

Finally we made it to our condo and headed in to check out the rooms. Dad began unloading the suitcases and told us to change into our swimsuits.

We all had on our swimsuits under our clothes and were ready in ten seconds.

"Hold on just a minute," said Dad, smiling. "Why was I not notified of this plan?"

"Because you may have told us not to do it," said Amy.

"We just wanted to be ready faster," said Shannon.

"Be prepared, is my motto," I volunteered.

It took Dad forever long, but finally we were on our way down to the pool. We had noodles, towels, and the dreaded sunscreen covering our skin.

The elevator was very slow to get to our tenth floor and then proceeded up to the eighteenth floor before descending. Then it proceeded to stop on every floor, even though the floor lights were not lit.

"What is going on with this elevator?" asked Dad. "It seems to have a mind of its own."

Uh-oh.

I looked around and saw no little leprechaun, but I knew he was there. This was right up his alley to torture us like this. Just as we reached the second floor, we began going up again. We stopped on every floor, and sometimes there were people waiting to get on and sometimes there weren't.

"I think this elevator is playing an early April Fool's Day trick on us," my dad said.

Finally we were on the ground floor, and after investigating the lobby, game room, and restaurant, we made it out to the pool. I had seen the cool waterfall flowing into the pool from our balcony, but it was much larger now that we were standing beside it. There was a cool curvy slide and islands you could swim up to and sit on.

I was standing on the edge, about to jump in, when a blond girl came walking up to me.

"Hi," she said. "My name is Chloe, and I am eight today."

"Oh, well, happy birthday. My name is Jason, and I will be nine in a few months."

"I have a friend named Mary who is sitting over there. She thinks you are cute."

I looked over where she pointed, and saw only a girl sitting in a chair holding a Hillary Duff magazine in front of her face.

"She is a little shy," said Chloe.

Suddenly, somehow, my feet went out from under me, and I fell into the pool. I landed just in front of this really fat kid, who was not amused.

Everybody around began laughing, except the fat boy. Looking at his face, I felt my days were numbered.

"Sorry. I did not mean to do that," I offered.

"Yeah? Well, I think you did," he retorted. He seemed to grow taller right in front of my eyes.

"Yeah, Dad, here I come," I yelled to the imaginary voice calling me. Gotta run.

I could feel the glare of the fat kid and hear the laughs of the two girls. I swam over to Dad and my sisters, who were still laughing.

Thanks for the support, I thought to myself.

"That was so funny, Jason," said Shannon. "You looked like a real klutz."

"I do not think that fat kid thought it was funny," Amy said.

"Me neither."

"So what was that girl saying?" asked Shannon. "I think she was flirting with you."

"She was not. She just, uh, wanted to know where the Coke machine was."

Boy, I sure wish my friends would get here. I need some backup.

I swam to one of the islands, tried to get up to sit, and fell back into the water.

And who do you think just happened to be swimming by?

Yep, you got it.

The fat kid. The tall, big fat kid. The more I looked at him, especially so closely, I began thinking that he had more muscles than fat.

He came up coughing, looked at me with pure fire in his eyes, and calmly asked if I was looking for trouble or just as clumsy a nerd as I looked like.

"Just having some balance problems," I said. "Must be the medicine."

"What medicine?" he asked suspiciously.

My mind froze and I went blank. I could not think of a single name of a medicine, and I suddenly heard the words "For PMS," coming out of my mouth.

"What?" The fat kid roared in laughter. "Kid, you need to go have a talk with your mommy. And next time you come within ten yards of me, you will be sorry. Got it?"

I got it loud and clear. I swam the other way, embarrassed by my medical term—and I did not even know what it meant. I had heard it on television enough times, but apparently it was not a good answer.

I swam by the corner, and sitting there in the little indention for the filter, was Paddy O'Rourke. He was laughing so hard he could hardly contain himself.

"So what is PMS anyway?" I asked. "I heard you whisper that into my ear. I thought you were supposed to be helping me, not making me look like an idiot."

"Ah, 'twas but a wee bit of trickery. Just can't help meself sometimes. The look on yer face was priceless, laddie."

"I suppose it was you who pushed me in as well?"

"'Twas indeed, sure and begorra. And I was sitting on top of the elevator making you go up and down. I could hear ye through the vents, and all of ye crowded into that cramped space, complaining so loudly, was priceless."

More laughs followed. I noticed Paddy had a little mask around his neck, a scuba tank on his back, and fins on his feet.

"What are those for?" I asked.

"'Tis almost time for Sea Lady to pick me up. We have a date to go dolphin diving for a wee bit. She takes me down to the sunken ships and we look for lost treasure chests. 'Tis one of me favorite things to do."

"You are going to ride a dolphin named Sea Lady down to sunken treasure ships? You know the dolphin's name? Can she speak to you?"

"Shhh, don't be speakin' so loudly, me lad. 'Tis always a good chance ye may have somebody listenin' to yer conversations."

I looked around, but nobody was close.

Never mind the fact that I looked pretty silly standing in a pool looking into a drain.

"Well, I am glad you had fun making me look clumsy, and I just hope you are around in case that fat kid decides to pounce on my head."

Paddy laughed and said not to worry. He had to run, as Sea Lady was waiting for him about twenty yards out from the beach. I strained to look over the flowers around the pool, and out in the ocean I saw a dolphin jump out of the water.

"There's me ride, laddie. We'll talk more later." With a smile, he removed his pointed little green hat, rolled it carefully, and slipped it into a tiny tube. He bowed deeply and was gone.

Chapter Three

When we got back up to the room, Mom had unpacked and organized everything. Jennifer was begging for a snack, and since we all were starving, we popped popcorn and watched TV for a while. Then we all had to shower and get ready to go to the store and buy groceries. It was pure torture to pass all the tempting rides and golf courses, but Mom assured us we would go the next day. As we walked through the store, I volunteered to go pick up the cereal of all cereals, Fruit Loops. I was suddenly hit in the back of the head by a strawberry. *Where did that come from?* I looked around, expecting to see the fat kid.

Worse.

Much worse.

It was the bratty cousins, Greg and David.

Oh no. Mom had assured all of us that they were in another part of the city, far, far away.

"What are you guys doing here?" I calmly asked.

"We had an accident in our condo, and since they were all booked, they moved us to another condo down this way."

"Oh," I said. I am sure the color was draining from my face. All my plans of glory and fun quickly disappeared.

"Well, maybe I will see you around," I said.

I calmly walked around the corner, and then I took off to find the rest of the family. Next time I will not venture off on my own to find the Fruit Loops.

"Mom," I gasped, "I just ran into Greg and David. They are here, staying near us."

"Oh no," groaned Shannon and Amy.

I think even Mom and Dad groaned as well.

"My sister tried to call me, but I missed the call and have not checked my voicemails,"

Mom said. She quickly pulled out her cell phone and dialed.

We all watched her closely, then on the next aisle we heard her sister answer the phone. We all walked around to the next aisle, and there they all stood.

Aunt Nancy came over and hugged Mom and Dad and each of us. Then she quickly explained that something had gone wrong with the fire sprinklers in their condo and it had some water damage. "So they had to move us, and now we are in another condo at this end of Destin."

My mind began to think of all the ways Greg and David could have broken the sprinkler system.

"Which condos?" I asked hopefully.

"Destin Plaza Towers," she said.

I am sure we all went pale.

"Which one are you guys in?"

"Same one. Which floor?" Dad asked.

"Eleventh. Eleven twenty."

And we were ten twenty. They were staying directly over our condo. My stomach was churning at the thought of one whole week with them.

I looked over at them, and they were smiling sweetly at me.

For a moment, nobody spoke. Then Aunt Nancy said, "But I have booked us several day trips on fishing boats and snorkeling boats, so you may not be seeing much of us."

It was a very small comfort that Aunt Nancy, Mom, and Dad all knew that the antics Greg and David had played on the ski trip made them less than ideal companions for another vacation.

A mere glimpse is too much, I thought.

We finished our shopping, loaded back into the van, and we all spoke at once. Shannon, Amy and I began voicing our concerns in a somewhat frenzied panic.

Mom and Dad told us to calm down, that they would go out of their way to make sure none of the bad things that happened on the ski trip with Greg and David the past winter would happen on this trip.

"I have some day trips that we can do as well," she assured us.

Chapter Four

That night Dad took Shannon and me down to the game room. We each were allowed to use our own money, up to five dollars. I played several games but was not much in the mood. My friends were coming in the morning—and not a minute too soon to suit me.

I woke the next morning with no cover and was freezing. The air conditioner must be directly over my bed and was surely set at zero. I looked around for my covers and found them on Shannon and Amy in the next bed.

I whipped my sheet and blanket off them, which somehow hurled them to the floor.

"Ow!" they screamed. Then they screamed at me some more.

Mom and Dad ran in and found them on the floor as mad as I have ever seen them. They both pointed at me with fingers ready to shoot me.

"What happened?" Dad asked

"Nothing, I just pulled my sheet and blanket off, because I am freezing. They stole it from me in the night."

"We did not," they protested.

"Then why is your sheet and blanket on your bed and you are holding theirs?" Mom asked.

Uh-oh, not again! I seem to remember this same event happening last Christmas Eve when Shannon was sleeping in my room. I knew this was a battle I would never win.

"I guess I was dreaming. I am very sorry, girls."

"Sorry enough to pay for our putt-putt golf and ice cream today?" they asked.

I looked at Mom and Dad for help, and they said nothing.

"How about a double scoop ice cream with sprinkles?" I negotiated.

"Okay, that works."

I think that is what they wanted all along. Girls are good at that kind of stuff.

The next morning, which was really just a few hours later, we ate our favorite vacation breakfast of Fruit Loops and blueberry muffins, then we headed down to the beach. We had packed a cooler of drinks and fruit and sandwiches. Sunscreen was no doubt in there also.

My dad had bought some cool things to hold down beach towels so they would not blow away. They were called Towel Traps. We each had our own set of four, so we laid out our new towels and anchored the corners. I was not one to lie much on the beach, but I knew I would need it to eat on. We headed out to the water, and people started yelling about dolphins out there. We all watched them for about twenty minutes until they swam away. I wondered if Paddy was riding one of them. One dolphin in particular kept swimming right in front of us.

"I bet that is Sea Lady," I said aloud without thinking. Suddenly a Frisbee hit me in the back of the head. I did not need to look around to know who sent it aloft in my direction.

I turned anyway and saw a little boy about six running over.

He apologized, and as he took back his Frisbee, I noticed it said Notre Dame on it. My fears were getting the best of me. I had expected to see the muscular fat kid had thrown it directly at my head, but I now knew Paddy had directed it my way as a reminder not to talk about Sea Lady or other secrets. Grampa had told me right after Christmas that if Paddy ever wanted to let me know he was around, or if I needed any reminders, his signal was anything about Notre Dame.

We had our boogie boards with us and were soon in the water riding the waves.

Not long after, Jack and Bobby arrived and ran down to where we were sitting, and I felt much relief. At last I had some comrades.

We went out to swim, and I told them about the girls, and the fat kid, and the bratty cousins.

"Aw, man, that's awful," Jack moaned.

We were laying on our stomachs on the boogie boards, looking down at fish and stuff, when suddenly I was overturned and dumped into the water. I came up sputtering and was face to face with the perpetrator.

The fat kid.

"Oh, excuse me I must have lost my balance. Must be the medication I am taking." He laughed and swam away.

"Let me guess, that is the fat kid," said Bobby.

"Yep."

We decided to go up to the pool, and of course the two girls I had met yesterday were there. Now I could see the face of the one who had been hiding behind the magazine yesterday. She also had blonde hair. But we did not have much interest in them. We practiced our swim team laps of butterfly, backstroke, freestyle, and breaststroke. Then, to really be cool, we each did an IM. That stands for individual medley where you swim four laps consecutively, each lap using a different stroke.

They seemed duly impressed, even though we did not really care, and swam over to us while we rested.

We talked, found out where they were from, and then they groaned.

"What?" we asked.

"Here comes that fat kid. He is nothing but a big bully who likes us," said Chloe.

"Yeah, he keeps staring at us and trying to impress us by flexing his muscles," said Mary.

"Those are really muscles?" I asked.

We all laughed, and the guy stopped, sat in a chair, and glared at us.

Suddenly a sea gull flew over and dumped right on his head.

"Ahhhhha," he said. He grabbed his towel and tried to wipe it off, but it was no use. He stoically got up and strolled to his room. Before he got to the door, the person who must have been his mom ran over and began rubbing his hair. Apparently she had seen what had happened. This lady had on a hot pink swimsuit with huge pelicans on it and a little short skirt that stuck out around her like an inner tube. It must have been the size of her body, because those pelicans looked life-size to me.

We all watched in shocked silence before we collected ourselves. Nobody said it, but I was sure were all thinking how glad we were that our moms did not dress like that.

It was bad enough to have a bird poop on your head, but to have your mom run over like that was worse.

We were still talking when suddenly two cannonball splashes landed beside us in the water.

The girls screamed, and we all turned to see the bratty cousins.

"Aren't you going to introduce us, Jason?" Greg asked.

"These are my...cousins, Greg and David," I told the girls.

"Nice to meet you," they said, looking like they did not mean it at all.

"We just got back from putt-putt and go-cart racing," David said. "It is really cool because we can drive so fast. And we had nearly perfect golf games."

"Perfect?" I asked.

"Yep, these courses are way too easy for us."

"Who wants to challenge us to a putt-putt match?" asked David.

All looked at me, and I suddenly noticed my arm was raised.

Oh no. Not again. How is it possible that my arm is raised once again without my knowledge?

Paddy O'Rourke.

"Okay," said David. "What is your bet?"

"We bet that each one of us, including Shannon and Amy, can beat you at a game of putt-putt. And the losers have to serve the winners pizza down here at the pool tomorrow for lunch. Including soft drinks and cookies."

Greg and David looked at each other, laughed, and said it was a deal.

"And we like sausage, mushroom, and double cheese," they threw in.

Chloe and Mary asked who Shannon and Amy were.

"My little sisters," I said.

"Aren't those guys older than you all?"

That was already a concern to me, but I just had to hope that since Paddy had raised my arm for me, that he was willing to help us out.

"We have a secret weapon," I said, "and it is called good luck."

"I sure hope so," said Jack

We ran over to Mom and Dad and told them of our bet, and they agreed to take us in the morning.

Chapter Five

That night after dinner, we all went swimming in the pool until it closed. Rob, Kelly, and Patrick had arrived as well, and they joined us. After we were back in our condo, we got our pajamas on and we all sat out on the balcony eating popcorn and nachos. We watch some teenage girls and boys playing volleyball on the beach. There were two big lights at the edge of the pool deck shining on them. Then we saw the big kid. He seemed to appear out of nowhere, and he was sneaking down to watch the volleyball game. After about ten minutes, we saw something we had never seen before. We all stared in amazement as the fat kid's mom stormed around the pool, went to where this kid was hiding, grabbed his ear, and began practically dragging him back inside. She was yelling at him, and he was yelling back that she was hurting his ear and to please let go. The volleyball game stopped, as all watched this spectacle. His mom had on a huge hot pink fuzzy robe with polka dots on it, big pink fuzzy slippers, and her hair in pink curlers in a pink hair net.

Now this was a really big lady, who apparently loved pink.

"Wow," I said. "I'm so glad you do not dress like that, Mom."

"Me too," said Dad.

After they had gone inside, there was a moment of stunned silence, and the teenagers roared laughing and continued their game.

"Poor guy," said Shannon. "I feel sorry for him."

Even though I had already had several encounters with him, I also felt sorry for him.

"That was a good note to end the day on," Dad said, and we all went to bed.

The next morning, after breakfast, we all got dressed and headed for the putt-putt course. When we drove up, I was very pleased to see that the name of this course was The Luck of the Irish Putt-Putt.

Let's hope so....

My aunt Nancy sat with Mom and Jennifer while Dad walked and kept score. It was agreed that he was the official scorekeeper for such an important event.

Amy went first and got a hole in one on the first hole. Then Shannon got a hole in one. Then I did as well.

"Beginner's luck," Greg sneered as he and David both got two strokes.

It was not that easy on each of the following holes, but it surely was funny. We younger kids could do nothing wrong, and the bratty cousins could do nothing right. They exchanged their balls and putters several times, but nothing could keep their balls from wildly bouncing off the windmill arms on the third hole. No matter how hard they tried, their balls simply could not make it between the giant leprechaun arms swaying down on the sixth hole. Each hole we came to made them madder and madder. It was either nature, or animals, or wind, or just bad luck, but they found it impossible to make even close to par on every hole. Their balls spun around the holes then rolled away. They rolled up the green hills of shamrocks then back down again on hole number ten. They bounced from one potato to another in the field of potatoes on twelve, like a pinball machine, while our balls sailed smoothly right between the potatoes and into the hole.

At the fourteenth hole the wind began blowing Greg and David's balls back away from the holes, but not ours. It was so funny. They tried to predict which way the wind would blow from and block for each other, but it never worked. The wind always came from another direction and messed them up. And then a bird flew over and pooped on David's arm. As Greg was laughing at that one, another bird flew over and pooped on his shoulder.

"Ugh," they yelled. They stormed off to get some napkins from the concession stand and almost did not come back. Dad practically dragged them back and made them finish. At another hole, a frog kept jumping in front of their balls just as they headed for the hole. And even the sand was a problem for them. Sand suddenly blew onto the course and steered their ball away from the hole. It was an amazing thing.

The bratty cousins were beside themselves. They kept saying they had defective balls, or defective putters, but each one they exchanged them for was no better.

By the time we got to the eighteenth hole, we were all so far ahead that their heads appeared to be spinning. It was inconceivable that even four-year-old Amy had beaten them. My dad had to keep reminding them to quit yelling and act like good sports.

At the last hole they threw their putters and my dad walked over and made them pick them up and go apologize to the owner. That was doubly insulting since the owner was in the process of giving us all free passes to play again for our holes in one. Actually, we each had several holes in one.

After we finished, Aunt Nancy and the bratty cousins left, and we stopped by to get another ice cream.

Vacations sure were fun. I had to buy Shannon and Amy's as part of the blanket forgiveness, but it was such a fun day even that did not bother me.

At noon we all lined up our pool chairs to face the volleyball game going on at the beach. We were all anxiously awaiting Greg and David to begin serving us our winning bet lunch. Chloe and Mary came over, and we told them what had happened. They went back to the pool to watch.

A few minutes later, Greg and David brought us our pizza, drinks, and cookies. Aunt Nancy was behind them—to make sure they did not spit on it, I am sure. She told us the boys had just baked the cookies and that they were still warm.

I could see the looks of misery on their faces, and it was a wonderful thing. I knew I would probably pay for this moment, but for now it felt good.

"I wish those teenagers would let us play with them," I said to my friends as we ate.

"Maybe they will, if you ask," said Kelly.

"I doubt it, but let's ask," said Rob.

And so we did. The girls went off to swim with Mom and Dad and Jennifer, who was just learning. Shannon loved to help teach her to swim and to let her jump in to her.

"Sure," said the guy serving. "Just let us get two more points and win this game and we will let you guys join us."

Soon we were trying our hardest, but it was just too hard to keep up. The teenagers all played and served with less intensity, but we still had a hard time. We tried to learn how to set up the ball so other teammates could then spike it over the net, and that was sort of hard. We were getting better, but we could tell they wanted to get on with more challenging games, so we finished that game and left. They said they would let us play later and they would teach us some more game strategy.

We got our boogie boards and went to ride the waves—something we were better at. I was laying on my board, waiting for a wave, when suddenly I was once again flipped upside down. I came up, and while everybody around me laughed, I got back on the board. Suddenly Paddy was sitting on my board, out of sight from others.

"Sorry about that, laddie. Just couldn't help meself."

"Very funny," I said.

"Thanks for helping us out this morning at the putt-putt challenge," I told him. "It was great to be able to do everything right and for Greg and David to do so badly. They deserved it, I know, and it was so fun to watch. My dad said it was so unbelievable, he kept turning around to see if somebody from *America's Funniest Video* was filming us.

"'Twas nothing any good leprechaun worth his weight in gold wouldn't have done, me lad. Ye deserve to show off a little and put the cousins in their places. They get too big fer their britches sometimes and need to be brought back down to earth."

"Hey, Paddy, did you find any sunken treasure riding Sea Lady yesterday?"

"We found a German sub from World War II, but no gold. The sub was on an ocean shelf that shifted, ye know, so 'twas a bit nerve wracking for the Lady. We did not get too close. Dolphins have a natural sense of danger, and she won't take me anywhere dangerous for either of us. She said she would keep her eye on you all while you are down here this week."

"I saw some dolphins after you left. Was that you? What do you mean when you say she will keep an eye on us?"

"Sure and begorra. 'Twas me and Sea Lady. She is one of the most respected dolphins in the world. Ye don't know this, but she helps yer Navy and Coast Guard many a day. She saves thousands of human lives each year with her sense of sonar. And she saves many baby dolphins as well."

"How?"

"Well, sometimes if people are adrift in the ocean because of a shipwreck or storm, she will make a *ping* noise on the sonar screen until rescue boats arrive on the scene. And she sometimes jumps out of the water to make fishing or pleasure boats detour around while she is really keeping them from getting their nets or motors caught in abandoned fishing nets. And sometimes when ye kids are swimming near the beach, she will swim along the coast keeping the sharks away. She has raised her baby dolphins to be as watchful and helpful as she is, and she has a whole dolphin network around the world helping ye daily."

"Wow, I did not know. Can you tell me more about that?"

"Later, laddie, when we have more time. Gotta run." And he put on his mask and air supply and dove back into the water.

"There goes a dolphin," Patrick shouted. "Look how close—I cannot believe it."

I just stared in amazement. How I wanted to be able to ride a dolphin, especially with Paddy. I wondered what it would be like to know and be able to speak to a dolphin.

Jack and Bobby paddled over to me, and we watched the dolphin jumping in and out of the water. People had gathered on the beach to watch as well. Paddy and Sea Lady put on quite a show for us.

And to think, I was the only one in the world who knew that Paddy was riding on the fin of the dolphin and that she had a name, Sea Lady. And she protected people all over the world with her network of dolphins.

It was just too much to comprehend.

When Sea Lady finally swam off, we resumed trying out our luck at riding the waves. I was either not a good boogie board surfer or somebody kept flipping me over on purpose. Every time I got spilled into the swirling wave, I wondered if Paddy was making me fall into the water, or maybe the fat kid, or if I was just not good at this sport. It was always on my mind, and it gave me a lot to think about. Was I a klutz or not?

Chapter Six

That afternoon we all got our kites and began running down the beach to launch them into the wind. My dad was trying to help us with kite flying tips.

"Run into the wind, and let the string out a little at a time," he said. "If the kite begins to fall down, pull on the string to tighten the tension, and it should begin going up again."

We had over five hundred feet of string on each of our reels. Mine was the biggest dragon kite I could find. We had a great time picking them out, and each of the girls had one too.

Our goal was to have all nine kites flying at once. Even Jennifer had a Dora kite, while Shannon had a princess, and Amy had a butter-fly. Jack had Spiderman, and Bobby had a giant dinosaur. Kelly and Rob had picked out rocket ship kites that were really cool. Patrick's was a racecar.

It was very hard to watch where you were running, while watching the kite, as I found out when I suddenly fell face down in the sand.

"Owww."

I had run right over the fat kid, who had been asleep in a beach towel.

Oh-no, I thought as the kid jumped up and began yelling at me.

"You stupid little kid, are you trying to kill me?"

"No," I said as I wiped sand out of my mouth.

I could see his face turning red, and I had a sudden vision of being knocked down.

"I'm okay, Dad," I yelled over his shoulder.

I was glad that my dad was heading our way to check on me, because I could use that as a lifesaver, but I did not want him to come over to help me as this kid's mom had done when the bird pooped on his head.

The kid saw my dad heading over and silently began smoothing out his towel.

I helped with one side, said I was sorry, and began reeling in my kite, which was now lying on the sand far down the beach near another set of condos.

Whew, that was a close call, I thought.

When I finally got back with my kite, all the other kites were flying gloriously in the deep blue sky.

Everybody had had lots of time to laugh at me while I had been reeling in my kite, so I only had to endure a few chuckles.

I waited until I had a clear opening between the kites, then I once again tried to launch my dragon. It was pretty high up, but not all the way, when a sea gull ran right into my kite string.

Oh no, not again.

Down came my kite, spiraling like a spinning top. Going down fast, and it appeared to be heading toward...

Oh nooo....

How could this possibly keep happening?

And yet, there it was. Lying across his face.

The fat kid did not move for what seemed like a minute or two.

Then he jumped up and began tearing my kite to shreds.

"I do not know how you did that, kid, but it doesn't matter. You are either the bravest or the stupidest little kid I ever saw."

"I am really so sorry. I was not trying to hurt you. I do not know how all these things keep happening. Normally I am pretty coordinated and not a klutz like these past few days."

"Yeah? I do not believe you, but go back and play with your little friends."

"I really am sorry. What is your name?" I put out my hand and said, "My name is Jason."

He stared at me for a moment, then he said, "My name is Rodney."

After another pause, he shook it. I told him I would try not to fall on him ever again and walked back to where the others were.

That was the end of my kite flying for this vacation. I was beginning to feel sorry for Rodney, formerly known as the fat kid.

Everybody tied their kites to Mom and Dad's beach chairs, and we went to the pool

Chloe and Mary were swimming, and we began playing sharks and minnows. I saw Rodney walk up to the pool, and I yelled to him to join us. He looked startled that I would ask such a thing. He said that he had to go up to his room, but thanks anyway.

"Why did you ask him to play with us?" Bobby asked.

"Because I feel sorry for him. He has no friends here, an embarrassing pink mom, and I have managed to trip all over him for two days now. Maybe he seemed like a bully because he was lonely."

"Maybe," said Kelly. "But from the stories you guys have told me about what happened before I got here, I think you are just darn lucky he has not kicked your butt, Jason."

I nodded in complete agreement.

We continued playing for about an hour, and then we had to go in and get ready for dinner.

It had been a great day, mishaps and all.

Chapter Seven

That evening we went to a seafood restaurant. It overlooked the beach and ocean, and Mom let all us kids sit at our own table next to the railing, except Jennifer, who was too little

We were sitting there eating popcorn shrimp, hushpuppies, and French fries and watching the people on the beach.

Suddenly we heard a lifeguard running up the beach yelling to everybody to get out of the water.

"Sharks," he yelled.

We all dropped our forks and watched. We could see a fin barely visible in the evening dusk. And there were some teenage kids in the water.

"Out now!" the lifeguard yelled urgently while blowing his whistle.

I do not know why they could not hear him, but they were still in the water. They did not seem to notice all the commotion on the beach.

The lifeguard began running out into the water toward them, still blowing his whistle and waving his arms.

"Look!" I yelled. "A dolphin is coming to the rescue!"

The dolphin was jumping out of the water very close to the two boys, who were startled. Then the dolphin nudged their legs and they screamed in fear.

The shark turned to swim the other way. The boys never saw it though.

The lifeguard reached the boys and grabbed their arms to pull them toward the shore. He pointed to the shore, and they seemed more than willing to follow.

The boys were very scared, judging by the looks on their faces. They began talking furiously with their hands. Ah, sign language. They were deaf, and that is why they did not hear the lifeguard's yells and whistles.

They thought a shark had nudged their legs, but it was really the dolphin.

The lifeguard was trying to explain that the shark had already turned away from them and that it was the dolphin who had nudged them. The boys did not understand him, but soon a lady came running over. She was the mom of one of the boys, and she could hear what the lifeguard was saying and she translated into sign language and told the boys.

The relief was written all over their faces, but when they understood that a shark really was close to them, they shuddered.

The lifeguard began going further up the beach to get everybody out of the water in case the shark came back.

Everybody in the restaurant had been watching and began finishing their dinner.

"Wow," I said. "That dolphin saved those guys from the shark."

I knew it was Paddy and Sea Lady, but I could not tell anyone.

Except my Grampa Mac. He knows Paddy well and is the only person I am allowed to talk to about Paddy. I could not wait to tell him about this when we got home.

"That was amazing," said Bobby. "I would say that is a dolphin hero all right."

"She sure is a hero," I said proudly. I felt like I had been a part of it just because I knew what really happened. It was just as Paddy told me; Sea Lady was saving lives

"How do you know the dolphin is a girl?"

"Oh, just a feeling I have…."

After dinner, we headed over to the go-cart track. They were small go-carts but still looked like fun. We had to wear helmets, and we had the speed of snails, but it was still fun. Shannon was in the lead, and she must have had the fastest go-cart since none of us could seem to pass her. That was humiliating.

To make matters worse, when we came to a stop, I took off my helmet and goggles and everybody began laughing at me.

"What? I tried to go around her, but my go-cart was not as fast as hers."

They kept laughing and pointing at me. "Look at your face and clothes," they said.

I looked down, and apparently Shannon's go-cart had sprayed black spots of oil all over me.

Ugh. This was a revolting development. The oil was not to come off easily, and I had visions of my mom trying to use baby wipes on my face and arms. And my legs, I noticed. I was covered in oil spots.

Yep, here she came. Baby wipes in hand.

I wondered where I could run to, but just as Rodney had been caught, so was I.

Mom began wiping and I was the amusement once again. I was beginning to think that the only reason I was on this trip was for the amusement of others.

While Mom was wiping, I looked at the go-cart Shannon had been in. It was number eight—easy to remember, since that is my age.

We headed back to the hotel. I had to change clothes and take a shower. At least my hair had been covered by the helmet and the goggles had saved my eyes. Now I know why I thought the track lights had dimmed. My goggles had been sprayed with tiny specks of black oil.

Dad had taken the goggles to the track manager, and he was pulling the go-cart off the track as we drove off.

To top things off, my mom contemplated making me take my clothes off for the ride back to the hotel, but after my pleas, she agreed that I could not walk up to our condo in my underwear.

Can you imagine the humiliation of walking through the lobby to the elevator and running into Chloe? Or Mary? Or Rodney? Or the bratty cousins?

I promised to sit still and reminded her that no oil had seeped onto the back of my clothes.

After I showered, I went down to join Mom and the girls at the pool. My friends were back and joined us also. Their moms sat talking with my mom, and at times I was sure their laughter was at my expense.

The teenagers had once again begun a marathon of volleyball

After playing several games of Marco Polo, we pulled some chairs over and watched the volleyball. It was already dark, and I knew we would not be allowed to play with them tonight.

They had been joined by some more guys and some girls, so I was pretty sure they did not want us hanging around. I had learned some of their names. The girls I knew were Paige, Sarah, Angela, and Teresa, and the boys were Joseph, John, Stephen, Vanya, Dustin, and Ethan.

Soon we had to go upstairs, and we knew we would be allowed to watch them some more from the balcony.

After getting our pajamas on, my friends came and sat on our balcony with us. We ate potato chips and dip and dill pickles, which we also dipped into the French onion dip. The girls thought that was gross, but we men loved it.

My mom had just opened her book to read when suddenly a huge, hairy black spider the size of a tennis ball swung down at her. The screams could be heard about two miles away, I was sure.

My dad swatted it away with his flip flop, and it swung right back at him. We all screamed again, and we all flailed our arms wildly. I am sure we were quite a sight to all those down on the beach and at the pool who were now staring at us.

Suddenly the spider began going up, and Dad had a brainstorm. He grabbed it with his bare hand, and Mom yelled to him to drop it because it may be poisonous.

"Calm down everybody. Calm down," he said loudly. "It's a fake," Dad yelled over our screaming.

Silence.

We all looked up at the balcony above and knew instantly what had happened and who the culprits were.

The bratty cousins were at it again.

Mom said she would take care of this, and she went out the door to go see her sister.

When Mom walked into their condo, they were all laughing so hard that soon my mom joined in. Soon they all had tears in their eyes and could barely catch their breath. Aunt Nancy, Greg, and David were holding their stomachs and could hardly speak. My mom finally got the story. They had bought this huge hairy rubber spider at a gift shop down the road and then put it on a clear fishing line to drop down to our balcony.

They all walked down to our condo, and when they walked in, all four still laughing, we all began to laugh as well.

"We could just imagine you all flailing your arms and screaming," Aunt Nancy said. "We only wished we had been down at the pool so we could have seen you."

"My dad looked really funny when he swatted it away and it swung back by his face," I said.

"Did not scare me a bit," Dad said.

"Did too," we all yelled in unison.

Soon we all were laughing again. It was a fun evening. They stayed with us and we played Yahtzee until midnight.

At some point we started talking about the shark and dolphin we saw at the restaurant. Aunt Nancy was fascinated, but Greg and David were skeptical. They did not believe my parents when they said my recollection was accurate.

I wanted so badly to say more, and even say that the dolphin was most likely named Sea Lady, but I had been sworn to secrecy. If I slipped and said more than I should, something usually stopped me.

Like the Notre Dame Frisbee hitting me on the back of my head on the beach.

I did not want the dice to suddenly spring up and hit me in the forehead, so I kept quiet.

It really is a hard thing to keep so much knowledge trapped inside your head, especially for an almost nine-year-old kid

My mom got up to get a drink, and on her way back she flipped on the ceiling fan switch.

Suddenly my Sprite splashed and went everywhere on the table.

I said sorry and began wiping it up.

"A little clumsy, aren't you?" asked Greg.

"I guess so," I said.

But I knew better. This had happened once before on the ski trip.

I went into the bathroom to wash my hands, and I was right.

Paddy was sitting in the sink, mad as a hornet.

"Woe is me. Me hat is wet and sticky, and so are me knickers and me boots. Sure and begorra, 'twas the second time I lost me balance and fell into yer drink. And I was having a jolly time, sitting with Lily on the ceiling fan blades watching ye play Yahtzee. Lily loves to watch ye play, and she still has the quick reflexes to not be thrown off when the fan is turned on."

"'Tis me young age and quick reflexes," said Lily as she appeared on the counter.

"Hi, Lily," I said. "I am glad you did not fall into a drink. I have not seen you for a long time."

She blushed and said she had been very busy traveling around the world. She works with Sea Lady and her dolphins.

"You do? Paddy did not tell me that. It was Sea Lady who saved those deaf boys today, wasn't it?"

"Sure and begorra, 'twas her. Dolphins have an incredible sense of danger and of human life. She could also tell that the boys were deaf and could not hear the lifeguard yelling to them. That is one of the ways that dolphins and whales save human lives. They draw attention to the person in distress, and if that doesn't work, they call on us leprechauns to magically whisper into the ear of somebody who can help."

"Like when Paddy somehow whispered 'PMS' into my ear in front of the fat kid?"

"Ye didn't do that, did ye, Paddy? Oh, ye are a bad one. Just for that I shall not cook yer favorite meal for two whole weeks."

"No Irish stew and apple pie?" whined Paddy.

Lily winked at me and we both shook our heads no, as if we had a secret agreement.

Lily laughed as Paddy tried to clean the sprite from his clothes and hat.

The hat was really what bothered him most, since everybody knows a leprechaun loves his hat more than anything. Except his family and pot of gold, that is.

"Jason, it's your turn," my mom yelled.

"Coming."

"I wish I could see her and be able to talk to her. I cannot imagine how a dolphin can be so smart."

"She is truly one of the most beloved sea creatures in the whole world. She is incredible, and we are blessed to have her," said Lily.

"We will see you soon," said Paddy, and he bowed deeply, slapped his wet hat on his head, and they both were gone.

Chapter Eight

That night I fell asleep very quickly. It had been a long and exciting day. I began dreaming, or was it really just a dream?

Paddy was on my pillow whispering into my ear.

Or was he?

Was this part of my dream?

"Wake up, ye little sleepyhead. Ye have an adventure to go to before the morning sun rises."

"What?"

"Shhh. Don't wake the others. I just did not want to alarm ye by wakin' ye up out on the beach."

"What?"

"Okay, just close yer eyes, and when ye wake up again, you'll understand."

I closed my eyes and I thought I was beginning to dream again. Until I felt cold water on my feet, that is.

"Yow, that's cold," I yelled. "Where am I?"

"Yer on the beach, laddie. And ye have on a mask and diving gear. Yer goin' on a ride with me and Sea Lady. 'Tis the first of many secret adventures of yer lifetime."

"What?"

"Still half asleep, are ye? Well, this will snap ye out of it and into the present quite quickly."

He snapped his fingers, and a little crab appeared and nipped slightly on my toe.

"Ow! What was that?" I jumped up and down a few times.

"Now ye seem to be fully awake, sure and begorra. Now listen up. Sea Lady is right in front of us, and she agreed to trust both of us enough to take ye on a magical ride tonight."

"A ride on Sea Lady? But I do not even know how to use this diving equipment."

"No problem, laddie. Ye just put this mask over yer eyes and put this mouthpiece in yer mouth and breathe normally. This is magic human equipment, and ye don't have to be certified to use it."

"Is Sea Lady going to talk to me?"

A voice from the water answered me.

"Yes, Jason, I will talk to you throughout the trip. You will be able to understand me under the water as well."

"Oh wow," is all I could manage to say.

"Let's go."

I walked into the water up to my waist, and I felt Sea Lady. She was smooth and I rubbed her gently. I had never touched a dolphin before. I did not want to stop rubbing her thick skin. I could see the wet, shiny outline of her sleek body in the bright moonlight. My fingers felt like magic on her fin. I did not want this moment to stop.

Was this all a dream? If so, I did not want to wake up for a long time.

Suddenly my mask and mouthpiece were on, and Paddy and I were sitting on Sea Lady. The moon was out, the stars were shining brilliantly, and we skimmed across the ocean. It was the most fun I ever had.

"When you feel comfortable, we will dive down and I will show you some real ocean treasures," said Sea Lady.

We splashed and jumped through the water for quite a while. Then Sea Lady slowed and asked if I was ready to dive.

"Sure, I think so," I said.

As Paddy and I held on effortlessly, we went deeper and deeper down into the ocean. It was dark outside, but somehow I could see everything very clearly. The ocean seemed to have a magical spotlight down there, just for me. It was the most beautiful place I had ever seen. The ocean floor seemed like a stage. There were large and small starfish, crabs with giant shells strolling along, sea urchins waving gently, jellyfish slowly floating by, and even a beautiful mermaid. Many kinds of sharks, baby dolphins, and even barracudas swam by us. There were bright pink coral formations and huge boulders that seemed to be home for many of the fish. I felt like I was sitting on the front row of a magnificent marine life production, and we were the guests of honor. The most beautifully colored fish swam by us and seemed unafraid. In fact, it was almost as if all the sea creatures bowed in respect to Sea Lady.

We paused at the bottom of the ocean, and Paddy waved to a huge octopus. The octopus waved back with all his arms.

"That's me friend Ollie," said Paddy somehow.

How could I hear underwater?

Suddenly an octopus from the other side of us reached out and pulled off Paddy's hat.

"Sure and begorra, Oscar, ye have two seconds to replace me hat before I turn ye into a squid."

Oscar and Ollie, it turns out, are longtime friends of Paddy and love to tease him with his hat. As everyone knows, even marine life, a leprechaun's hat is his prized possession.

"'Tis the reason I usually take the time to roll up me hat and stuff it into me tube," said Paddy.

Oscar replaced the hat gently, seemed to smile at me, and floated off.

We swam on and came up to a sunken German submarine that had been there since World War Two. It was covered with sediment and barnacles and was barely recognizable. Sea Lady would not take us very close since it was dangerous.

"That is the sub we saw earlier," said Paddy. "'Tis not safe to go near, 'tis unstable."

I was hoping this was not just a dream, but if it was, it was the most amazing experience of my life. I wanted this moment to last forever.

But soon we came up and gently floated on the surface of the ocean. Small waves rocked us gently as we talked.

"What do you think about my world, Jason?" Sea Lady asked.

"I think it is the most beautiful place in the world. Thank you for showing it to me."

"Paddy thinks very highly of his McLaughlin laddies."

"Yer Grampa Mac and his father Leo loved the ocean also."

"Grampa Mac has been on a trip like this too?"

"Sure and begorra, when he was a lad nearly yer age," said Paddy.

"I have known the McLaughlin clan for many years. Even though your last name is not McLaughlin, you are strong enough and conscientious enough that you have been entrusted with this wonderful gift. The leprechauns have been helping the human race for thousands of years using a network of whales and dolphins. Not too many people know about this, since it is such a highly secretive mission for us. That is a lot to carry on your young shoulders, Jason, but we know that you are up to it."

"How can I help you, Sea Lady?"

"By always being honest, hard working, responsible, loyal, and kind. The rest will come to you. You will always know what is the right thing to do," she said.

"'Tis getting late, so I must get ye back to yer bed before sunrise," said Paddy.

"Good night, Sea Lady. And thanks for the best trip of my life. I hope we meet again, and I will always try to help you all."

"Thank you, Jason. Good night."

As I stood watching her swim away, I was suddenly back in my bed, in my dry pajamas, with my hair dry. I closed my eyes, and tried to absorb it all.

Chapter Nine

"Wake up, Jason!" yelled Amy as she jumped on my bed. "We are going out on a snorkeling boat to a cool island today."

"Okay, just a minute."

I wanted to lie there and see if I remembered my trip in all the color detail. I wanted everything to remain etched in my brain forever.

"What time do we leave, Mom?" I yelled.

"After lunch, at one o'clock," she yelled back.

Good. I had lots of time to lie here and think. But I did not want to lie there and think. I wanted to go out in the ocean and think.

I got up, got my swim trunks on, and went into the kitchen to eat some Fruit Loops.

"Did you sleep well?" Mom asked.

"Yes, I slept great."

I ate quickly and called Jack and Bobby's rooms to see if they were up and wanted to go walk on the beach early. Dad wanted to go too, so we did not have to wait until the girls got ready. I will never understand why girls have to fix their hair and why Mom has to put on her makeup before going down to the pool and beach. It's all gonna wash off the first time they get wet anyway, but that does not deter them.

Soon we all met up and began walking. We found some great shells, and each one reminded me of the crabs walking on the ocean floor. We also found some starfish, and I said, "I bet there are a lot more out there, in all sizes."

"Yeah, I bet the ocean gives us just a small sample of her beauty," said Dad.

I couldn't have said it better myself.

We walked back to our chairs and got our boogie boards. Dad sat on the lounge chair and began reading the newspaper they leave outside our door each morning.

We were floating around on the water, talking and enjoying the waves when we could catch one. They were coming faster and larger than the last few days, so we were being bounced around a lot. There were a lot of people, adults, teenagers, and kids in the water enjoying the stronger waves. It seemed like the lifeguard was walking up and down the shore more often also. As we watched him, we saw a little boy run up to him with a cut on his foot. He probably stepped on a shell, we said. The lifeguard went back to his stand and got out his first aid kit to bandage it for him.

I glanced toward the shore and saw a frightful sight.

The fat kid, or the muscular kid, was running quickly down the sand and toward me in the water.

Oh no, I thought. *He is coming to try and dunk me again, and I thought we had an agreement of sorts, after our handshake.*

No, he dove into the wave about fifteen feet from me and began swimming like an Olympian. I turned to watch, since he had on his shorts and shirt and sandals. Then I saw her.

A girl was floating face down in the water.

Rodney reached her, grabbed her under her arms, and swam back to shore. Even though she was older than him, he carried her with ease and ran to the sand and laid her down gently.

"Jason, run get the lifeguard and tell your dad to call 911," he ordered.

I ran to Dad and told him and he began dialing. I ran over to the lifeguard, who was still bandaging the little boy.

As we ran back, Rodney was doing CPR on the girl. He was counting out loud, and she was still not breathing.

"I think she had an epileptic seizure," he told the lifeguard.

"Thanks, I will take over now. Please stay in case I need you. You were doing a great job."

Rodney stepped aside and let the lifeguard take over the compressions.

Suddenly the girl coughed up some water and began choking. But she was finally breathing.

Her eyes looked funny, and she began shaking.

"She has a bracelet on that says she has epilepsy," said Rodney, "and I recognize the symptoms. My little sister had it too."

"Does anybody know where her mom is? Or which room she is in?"

"She is two doors down from me," said Jack. "I will run up and knock on the door."

He took off, sand flying behind him.

A crowd gathered, and we all stepped back, following the lifeguard's orders.

"Did anybody call 911 for me?" asked the lifeguard.

"I did," said Dad.

We heard the siren, and Dad ran to guide them to her more quickly. Soon Jack returned with the girl's mom and dad.

"I just ran up to get the sunscreen," her mom screamed. "She is having a seizure, and I have her medication here."

The ambulance paramedics loaded her up and drove off, with her mom riding along.

"I think she is going to be just fine, thanks to you, son. What is your name?" asked the lifeguard.

"Rodney, sir."

"Rodney, you did an outstanding job of CPR, and I was told that you dove in to save her. I can tell, since you have on your shorts and shirt and sandals. That was a wonderful thing, son. Do you have any lifeguard training?"

"Yes, sir, I am a junior lifeguard at my pool. I have never actually saved anyone though."

"Well, for a first save, you did perfect. Your CPR technique was perfect, and you had 911 called and had somebody run to get me, so you followed procedures exactly. Congratulations."

"Thank you."

"That was amazing, Rodney," I managed to say. "You dove into the wave and swam like an expert."

"Thanks, I have been on a swim team at our club since I was five."

"Rodney, What is going on? Why are your clothes soaked and covered with sand? I am ready to leave for my appointment, and now I have to wait for you to change. What is wrong with you?" the pink lady was yelling suddenly.

"Ma'am, is this your son?" asked the lifeguard, pointing to Rodney.

"Yes, what has he done?"

"Well, ma'am, your son just dove into the ocean, pulled an unconscious girl out of the water, began doing CPR on her, and saved her life. I think his clothes will dry."

"Oh, well, in that case, you are excused, Rodney. Now go up and change so we will not be late for our fittings."

We all just stared at her. She had on an enormous pink straw hat and an equally enormous sundress that was, of course, hot pink. Even her sandals were pink to match her enormous pink pocketbook. Why, as I looked closer, her earrings were pink seashells and her necklace matched.

Rodney slowly turned to go change.

"And hurry it up," she yelled after him.

"Ma'am, do you understand what your son just did? He saved a girl's life. He had 911 called and had already sent somebody to find her mom and began CPR on her, all before I got here. Do you understand that your son is a hero? Don't you think a little praise is in order, rather than yelling at him for getting his clothes wet?" the lifeguard asked her.

"Yes, I understand, and I will speak to him later. Now if you will excuse me, I have an appointment for a fitting."

She turned and walked away as she burst into tears.

"Unbelievable," said Dad.

We all stood there, staring after her.

"When Rodney gets back, I am going to recommend that he gets an award for what he did. I don't think his mom appreciates his achievement at all," said the lifeguard. "I have to fill out the incident report and will get his name and address later. Thanks for your help, everybody. I think she will be fine, and I hope she will be out of the hospital soon."

We all began walking back to our towels now that the excitement was over.

"I feel so bad for Rodney. His mom acted like she did not care at all what he did and was so mad just because his clothes were wet," said Bobby.

"Like I said earlier, I am sure glad that is not my mom."

"Me too."

Dad just shook his head, trying to follow Mom's advice: If you can't say something good, say nothing at all.

"Well, we will have to make it a point to all congratulate him later."

"Congratulate who?" asked Mom as she and the girls joined us. "We just saw an ambulance leave, and came down to see what was happening."

We explained it all, and Mom said we should make him a cake or something.

"Yeah, let's make cupcakes and we can have a party for him tonight down at the pool."

"That sounds like a plan," said Mom. "You can buy what we need on the way home from the snorkeling trip."

Oh, I had forgotten all about that. Mom had booked a day trip for us to go out on a boat to a small island where they would give us snorkels and masks and we could float around for an hour or so observing the underwater world. Mom was not going with us, since she had to stay with Jennifer, so Dad had us all to himself.

Since the teenagers were probably all still sleeping, we had the volleyball net all to ourselves and we decided to make good use of it. We all practiced our serves, and Dad showed us how to set the ball up so that another teammate could hit it over the net. He taught us how to keep score, and we improved our skills from when we played with the teenagers last. We were all excited to show them our improvements.

My dad served, and my plan was to set it up for Jack. I intended to gently hit it straight up and step aside for Jack to smack it. However, the volleyball seemed to have a mind of it's own, and it went sideways. It landed squarely on the green hat of a man sitting in a beach chair attempting to drink his tea. The ball bounced off his head, knocked his drink out of his hand, and landed on his chair between his knees.

I ran over and apologized profusely.

He calmly smiled at me, began drying his body that was now covered with tea, and plumped up his hat. He had a reddish beard and hair to match.

"'Twas a thought in me head that it may be a wee bit dangerous to sit here, but I think life is a gamble anyway, so no worries, laddie. 'Tis not too much of a mess, and I was nearly through with me mornin' tea as it was."

I stared at him. The only person I had ever heard talk like this was Paddy, Huey, or Lily.

I wonder....

"My name is Oliver Paden, and what would ye be called?"

"My name is Jason."

I shook his outstretched hand, and he winked at me.

"Nice to meet ye, laddie. Now enjoy yer volleyball game, and don't give this mishap another thought. Things like this happen to me all the time. I would not know how to act if funny things did not happen to me. Ye know what I mean?"

I did, I really did, and I nodded.

Again, I wondered....

I ran back to the volleyball game, but my mind was on Mr. Oliver Paden from Ireland.

Chapter Ten

After lunch, those of us going on the snorkeling trip lathered on the SPF-thirty sunscreen, got our towels and flip-flops on, and headed to the car. We met my friends and their dads at the elevator to go down.

We got on rather quickly, then began going up. All the way to the top, floor by floor.

Oh my, not again. Apparently Paddy thought this was quite funny, and he was most likely sitting on top of the elevator laughing.

"What keeps happening to this stupid elevator? The floor buttons are not even lit, and yet it stops on every floor. Then it goes up just as we nearly reach the bottom. I am going to have to report it," said Dad.

Finally we all got off at the fourth floor and walked down the stairs. I am quite sure Paddy was having a grand time watching us and laughing.

All the way to the dock, I could not quit thinking about Mr. Oliver Paden. I was hoping to have time later to talk further with him. I keep wondering if he also has a leprechaun, or maybe knows someone who does.

Soon we arrived at the dock, and guess who else was there?

Yep. You got it.

Greg and David, the bratty cousins. Maybe, just maybe, they were not going to be on our boat.

Aunt Nancy ran over to us and said that they had planned on going on the nine o'clock outing, but the boat needed a repair so they booked them on this one. She did not know we were on this one as well. She whispered she was so sorry to Dad.

Great.

I put on my stoic not-to-worry face and pretended it did not matter.

The captain of the boat asked if we all had sunscreen on, and when we all nodded affirmatively, he handed out life jackets. Everyone, even parents, had to wear one.

Greg and David balked, said "These are for babies," and acted like they would not wear it.

Good, I thought. *Then maybe you will not be on this boat after all.*

We all boarded, and at the last minute they complied and stepped aboard.

The captain was an older man with weathered, deeply tanned skin. His face looked like he was bored. He checked his instruments, and we were off.

It was a two-hour ride to the spot we would be anchoring. Nearby this place was a little island with no buildings, just a thatched hut and picnic tables. The plan was to snorkel for an hour then go to the island for a snack and drinks, which appeared to be stored in three large coolers in the cabin..

Finally we reached the perfect location, according to the Skipper.

I think I forgot to mention that the captain of this boat asked us to call him Skipper. And we were all his first mates. Skipper gave us all masks and snorkels, mentioning to each parent that they had all been sterilized beforehand. I could see the look of relief on my Aunt Nancy's face from here.

Dads? Not so much into worrying about germs and stuff like that.

Greg and David both stood and prepared to jump in when the Skipper told them to sit back down. We had rules to go over before anybody touched the water.

I could not wait to see how the ocean looked from this view. No way it could look as magical as it did on my midnight dolphin ride, but I was still anticipating the beauty of it.

We all had our instructions, and when we heard the horn blow, we had to immediately get out of the water. He assured us that dangerous fish, including sharks, did not typically inhabit this location but we had to be careful anyway.

Skipper kept wiping his forehead, and seemed to be sweating a lot. He had a cloth that he dipped in the cooler water and applied it to his neck.

Dad told us that we all had to stay together, and we knew he meant business.

So we stayed together. That was good anyway since it kept us away from you-know-who.

Though the fish and water and coral were beautiful, it did not even compare with what I had seen before. We floated around, marveling at times when we all surfaced and exchanged 'Did you see that?' comments.

Soon we heard the horn and climbed aboard. As Skipper pulled up the anchor, we all talked at once about what we had seen.

"I saw a four-foot barracuda," said Greg.

"You did not. It was only two feet long," said David.

They argued back and forth until Aunt Nancy gave them the look. Then they resorted to punching each other.

Aunt Nancy rose to reposition herself between them and gave them each a pinch on the leg, which meant they should cut it out.

As we reached the island, Skipper again dropped anchor. He gave us all our marching orders. He appointed the strongest, including the three dads, to carry the coolers. Each of us had been designated something to carry ashore.

I received the first aid kit, and each other kid received a similarl size item. I think he must have been assigning every item that was not nailed down so that we each had an item to carry. Some carried such items as lanterns, which I saw no use for in the daytime.

Greg was assigned a small mirror, and David had the compass. Skipper put his cell phone in his pocket, and soon we were all sitting at the picnic tables.

Skipper began serving the food to all his first mates and told us about pirates and voyagers of the ocean. He said the lanterns and mirrors had often been used to guide rescue boats to stranded islanders. But sometimes they did not attract the rescuers. Sometimes they attracted pirates who came and robbed them.

"Then did they kill them?" asked Bobby.

"Sometimes they did, mate."

"Please tell us some of the pirate stories," said Shannon.

"Well, it was rumored that there had been a ship from France that sank in the Gulf not too far from here, on it's way to New Orleans. Supposedly had tons of gold to bring to the city for buildings and trade. But some pirates attacked it, and there was a fierce battle. The French ship sank, and for years the pirates fought over it."

"Did they ever find the gold?" I asked.

"Nobody knows for sure, but rumor has it that a pirate ship was captured, all the pirates had to walk the plank, and the ship was then towed away and burned afterward. No gold was found on it when they found the remains at the bottom of the ocean. So apparently the pirates kept stealing it from each other, and nobody really knows where it ended up."

After a few more stories, he explained what all the items were that we brought ashore and how they had been simple items that saved lives. It was amazing that these everyday items could be survival tools.

Soon he said that we better head back and for each one to carry the same item that he brought ashore. David and Greg were also assigned the trash bags, which they were not in the least happy about.

Skipper was the last to board, and as he reached the ladder, he collapsed and fell back into the water. Dad and Jack's dad jumped in and hauled him aboard. He was unconscious, and nobody noticed that his cell phone had fallen out of his pocket and floated away.

They laid him on the deck, and Dad asked somebody to get some water and a wet towel for his face.

"I'm sorry. I think the sun got to me for a second. I am all right," he said as he came to.

"Just lay there a minute and see how you feel," Dad said.

After a few minutes, he sat up and said he felt good enough to get us home. The men helped him to his captain's chair, where he started the engine after pulling up the anchor.

We backed slowly away from the small island, still thinking about the pirate stories.

Skipper told us to put all the items back exactly where they had been before, and explained why they had to be strapped down so that they would not be lost. Each of us took our turn, and we felt like we were actually real shipmates.

He showed us how to put the ship in different gears and how to use the compass in case we lost our navigation instruments. We were all studying the compass when Skipper reached for his radio. He began speaking, then suddenly collapsed, pulling his radio out of the cabinet with him.

Uh-oh. Dad and the other men picked him up, and this time he was unconscious. Dad reached over and turned off the engine. We all stared, and Dad asked if anybody knew CPR. Everybody said no.

I said, "Dad, I watched Rodney do CPR on that girl. I can help you."

Dad said "I do not think watching for a few minutes will help much. Let's get his cell phone and call for help first."

We searched his pockets, but no phone. We looked around the boat and could not find it anywhere.

"I saw him put it in his pocket before we went ashore," said Aunt Nancy.

"Yeah, me too," I added.

"Well, he must have dropped it in the water when he fell. Now none of us has our phone since we left all our clothes and personal items in the lockers by the dock. And the radio is not working now since he pulled it out of the cabinet when he fell."

"What do we do now?" Amy quietly asked.

"Let's think. First we try CPR and see if we can get him breathing."

"I know Rodney counted to fifteen, while pushing on her chest, then held her nose and blew into her mouth two times," I volunteered.

We began doing that.

"I also saw Rodney keep her head tilted back."

While Dad and I worked on the skipper, Jack and Bobby's dad began organizing.

"Okay guys, here is a plan. I will get the boat going again, heading north according to where the sun is heading. Who has the compass?"

"I will be in charge of the compass," said David.

"No, son, let me have that job."

David put it behind his back, and said, "I can do it. I promise I can."

"Son, let me have it. Please."

Greg reached behind his back to retrieve it, and David reacted violently. He swung his arm the other way, and away flew the compass.

Into the water, sinking immediately.

Uh-oh.

"Great. That was really smart guys. Now you both just sit there and don't move. Understand?"

They nodded slowly.

"Get the first aid kit and see if there is any aspirin in it," said Aunt Nancy. "If there is, put one under his tongue. It will help if it is a heart attack."

"Yeah, I remember reading about that," Bobby's dad said as he grabbed the kit.

He put an aspirin under the skipper's tongue as dad and I worked on him.

It was really hot, and we all began to sweat. "Better reapply the sunscreen," said Aunt Nancy.

Everybody except Dad and I—and, of course, the rebellious ones— did so. Greg and David said they already had enough on and wanted no more. Aunt Nancy was too tired and anxious to argue with them and let it go.

Had she known they had lied about putting it on earlier, she would have insisted.

The skipper moaned and was breathing. We stopped doing CPR, and he lay there, still unconscious but at least breathing. We put a towel under his head, as if making him comfortable would help bring him around.

"Okay, here is the plan again. I will head north as best I can, and you hold this mirror and try to signal any plane or boat you see."

He handed the mirror to Aunt Nancy.

It was really hard to keep our bearings because the sun was still not real low, but we had to be going somewhat north. Suddenly a dolphin jumped out of the water to our right. It jumped several more times, going away from us.

"Dad, follow that dolphin," I yelled.

I just knew that was Sea Lady guiding us home.

"What? Why would I follow a dolphin, Jason?" he asked.

"Because, I just know it. Look, I know it sounds crazy, but we are not heading exactly right, and we need to get him to a doctor the fastest way we can, right?"

The dads all looked at each other and looked back at me.

"Just trust me, Dad."

"Jason, I trust you, but how could you think that dolphin knows where we need to go?"

Suddenly I heard Paddy whisper into my ear.

"I watched a show the other day on TV. It was about dolphins somehow knowing or sensing humans need help and intuitively guiding boats with no navigational skills."

"Right, was that a science fiction movie?" Greg sneered.

"No, it was a real show, Dad, I promise. Can we just try it for a while? If the dolphin swims away, or appears to take us the other way altogether, we can go back to following the sun."

"Well, I do seem to remember that they had documented dolphin and whales seeming to act as guides," said Bobby's dad.

"Okay, what do we have to lose?"

So we headed off after the dolphin, who jumped up out of the water periodically.

About an hour later, Aunt Nancy noticed a small plane far off in the distance, and she began gently reflecting the sun toward it with the mirror.

"I wish I knew Morse code," she sighed.

"You're doing fine, Just keep it up. If nothing else, they may report us for being annoying."

The plane turned and headed toward us. We began waving our arms and pointing to the skipper lying on the deck.

The small plane tipped his wings and flew off.

"We did it," I yelled. "He has gone for help. Skipper taught us a survival tool, and we just needed to use it."

The dolphin was still guiding us, which surprised everybody but me. I was beaming with pride.

"Thanks Paddy and Sea Lady," I whispered.

Another fifteen minutes later, a Coast Guard boat pulled up beside us, where paramedics worked on Skipper. They gave him oxygen, and we told them we had put an aspirin under his tongue.

One of the officers remained on the boat with us after they took off with the captain, and he steered us home. The Coast Guard officer with us had boarded with a manual navigational system, as well as a phone system.

Soon we saw land, and we all cheered.

After we got off the boat, we all got our clothes and stuff out of the lockers.

"Well, that was sure an adventure," Dad said.

"Can we go ride go-carts now?" I asked.

Dad looked at his watch and said that we had time for a quick lap or two.

Greg sneered and said, "I bet you wish you could beat us."

"I will take that bet. I bet I can start off in front of you, stay in front, and never let you pass me," I said confidently.

"Yeah? Well, I say you can't."

"Another bet? Didn't you both learn your lesson on the putt-putt course?" Aunt Nancy asked.

Both boys glared at her for bringing that embarrassing subject up.

"We want to redeem ourselves," said David.

"Sounds good to me," said Dad.

We headed off to the same go-cart track we had been to before. While waiting in line, I looked for go-cart number eight. I remembered that had been the one that seemed the fastest and the one that had spit oil all over me. I assumed the oil leak had been fixed and was hoping they had not slowed it down in the process.

The men on the track waved all the go-carts to come in, and they slowly lined them up for our group. The gate to the track opened, and we all took off to find our perfect go-cart.

Number eight was in my sight. As I neared it, Greg dashed in front of me, heading straight for it.

Oh no, I thought. *I have a feeling I need that one.*

Suddenly Greg tripped on something, which slowed him down, allowing me to get into number eight.

"I wanted that one," he snarled at me. "Number eight is my lucky number."

"So sorry," I said.

After we all had been belted in and put on our helmets and goggles, the man in front of us read off a list of rules.

"No horseplay, no cutting in front of anybody, no bumping, no stopping on the track. Watch these flags. When I wave the yellow flag, it means slow down, and when I wave the red flag, it means to slow down and come in, that your ride will be over. If there is any dangerous driving, your ride will be over. Got it?"

We all nodded, I supposed.

"Good. Now watch the red light over here. It will flash from red to yellow and then to green. When you see the green, you can slowly, and I repeat slowly, take off."

I looked around to see where everybody was. Greg and David were behind me, glaring at me.

I smiled at them.

Shannon and Amy were in pink and purple helmets near the back. Amy was the youngest out there, and we were always watching out for her.

The red light countdown began, and at the split second I saw green, I floored it. I took the inside lane and kept myself focused. I knew Greg and David would be hot on my tail, trying everything possible to pass me. I could hear the roar of their go-carts as they tried to pass me, but I did not dare look around. Then I came around a curve and Amy was suddenly in front of me. I swerved a little to the right, and Greg swerved to the left and took the lead.

"Oh no," I said.

"Yes," shouted Greg, punching the air as if victory was already his. By the time I got back down to the inside lane, they both were ahead of me. I was quickly losing hope and could feel the money in my pocket melting away, just as the cheese melted on the pizza I would have to buy and serve to those bratty cousins tomorrow when they beat me to the finish line.

I could see Greg and David straining forward in their seats, like they could not see. They began slowing down and were furiously flooring their gas pedals, but I was catching up fast. Maybe I just had a boost of power, but in seconds I zoomed past both of them and had the lead again.

Then I saw it.

The man was waving the red flag for us to come in. The race was over, and I had won again.

"I will have my pizza at the pool again, and I would like it served at noon, please."

I looked more closely at them, and we all burst out laughing. They were covered from head to toe in oil spots. Their goggles, helmets, and clothes were all speckled.

"Obviously they did not fix the go-cart," Dad said.

My mom was not there with the baby wipes, so they had to use napkins to clean their faces.

To say that they were mad at both losing and being sprayed with oil was an understatement. Furious was more like it.

I smelled a little whiff of pipe smoke and walked over to the fence. Paddy was sitting on the post and spoke quietly.

"'Twas a good race, laddie. Ye handled the driving quite well."

"Thanks Paddy. I almost lost it, but somehow got the lead back. Did you help me?"

"Nay, ye did it on yer own. But sure and begorra, 'twas me sittin' beside ye. 'Twas quite a thrill."

"You cheated, Jason," David yelled. "You knew that your go-cart would spit oil on us and that our goggles would get so dark that we could not see."

"No, that happened to me, but we saw the man take the go-cart off the track to fix it. I thought it had been fixed."

"Yeah, right."

"A bet lost is a bet paid," said Aunt Nancy. "Your lunch will be served as requested tomorrow at noon. Right, boys?"

They both glared at her.

"Right," she said quite a bit more sternly.

"Right."

"Well, we better head home. It is getting late, and this has been one of the most interesting days of my life," said Dad.

Chapter Eleven

That evening after dinner, we all went back down to the beach. The teenagers were playing volleyball. On the way home Dad had stopped at the grocery store, and Mom and Shannon and Amy made cupcakes. We placed the tray on a table and waited to see if Rodney came down.

Just a few minutes later, Rodney did come out. He had on his swim trunks and a shirt and carried his towel.

"Hey, Rodney, come over here," I yelled.

When he approached, we all began clapping. He looked embarrassed, but pleased.

Mom told him that everybody at the pool and beach had been talking about his heroic save that morning and that we wanted to share some cupcakes with him.

Shannon passed out the cupcakes, Amy handed out cans of Coke, and Jennifer handed out napkins.

We had made two batches, and at the end of the volleyball game, we invited the teenagers up to join us. We all sat around talking with Rodney, and he told us how he had learned lifeguarding and CPR.

"Well, my parents have belonged to a country club since I was born, so I began swimming when I was two. I learned swimming from the club swim team, and then we had a pool at home as well. When I was five, my little sister Bridgette was born. She was eventually diagnosed with epilepsy and would have a lot of seizures. By the time I was ten, I had asked to take CPR and junior lifeguard training in case I ever needed to use it on her. Sometimes she would have seizures while swimming in our pool, so we always had to watch her carefully. One day she had the worst one ever, and Mom and I tried to save her, but she died."

We all sat in silence, and then he continued.

"Bridgette loved the color pink, and that is why my mom wears only pink. She is still mourning her death. Just before she died, Bridgette was a flower girl for my cousin's wedding. She had looked so special, and it was the happiest day of her life. After she died, my mom could do nothing but eat and cry. I was the same, and we both gained a lot of weight. My mom finally went to a grief support group, and they came up with a way to help her get through the depression. They suggested that she do something that made her think of Bridgette and smile. The memory of Bridgette walking down the aisle in her little flower girl dress, beaming from ear to ear, with ribbons in her hair, always made Mom smile. So she decided to begin designing flower girl dresses and satin ribbon hairpieces. She has not gotten past wearing all pink, as I am sure you all have noticed, but she is finally beginning to enjoy living again. I know she looks funny in her outrageous pink outfits, but I just try to remember how much she has suffered, and I know it will pass."

"What do you do to help her, and yourself, to get past the sadness?" asked Mom.

"I began swimming again, and I quit eating everything in sight. I am losing weight and working out with weights also. I rejoined the swim team at my school."

Ah, that explains it all, I thought. Sometimes those arms looked fat, and sometimes they looked muscular.

"Well, we are all very proud of you, Rodney," Mom said. "You saved that girl's life this morning. Maybe that will help ease some of your pain."

"My mom and I talked about it on the way to her appointment right after that happened. We came down here because she had twin flower girls in a wedding this weekend and she was here to do the final fittings. She is also doing the little girls' hair and putting the ribbons in, the same style that Bridgette wore. After we left the appointment, my mom cried for a long time. The wedding is tomorrow."

"Where is your dad?" asked Shannon.

"He died the year before Bridgette died. He had a heart attack."

Again, we all sat in silence, absorbing all this sadness.

"Well, tonight is a time for new beginnings and a time to celebrate," said Ethan. He was one of the teenagers. "We heard all about your save this morning, and we salute you. Would you kids like to play a few games of volleyball with us before it gets too late?"

We all jumped up and ran to the beach.

"Girls, come back here," Dad yelled to Shannon and Amy. "Let the boys play with them."

The girls sat for a while pouting but soon got up to swim in the pool.

We had a great time playing volleyball. The practice with Dad earlier helped us play much better.

As we changed sides of the net, I noticed Mr. Oliver Paden was sitting in the same chair, facing the ocean, with his back to us. He was holding his hat instead of wearing it, I noticed with a smile.

Smart man.

After a few more minutes, Mr. Paden got up, watched us for a few minutes, and walked up to the pool. He put his green hat on as he passed us.

Since there was something about him that fascinated me, I watched him closely. He headed for a pool chair near the entrance to the pool and sat down.

Maybe I watched him a few seconds too long, since the volleyball had just bounced off my head.

"Ow," I said, rubbing my head.

"Pay attention," said Bobby.

That sounded like a good idea to me also.

We finished that game, and Dad yelled to us to give the teenagers their time alone now, so we headed to the pool for our games of sharks and minnows. This time Rodney joined us all, and we had a great time.

We were taking a break when Rodney's mom, formerly called the pink lady, came into the pool gate. As she fumbled with the gate handle, and her towel and room key, she suddenly tripped.

Mr. Paden jumped to his feet and caught her just as she was about to hit the concrete.

"Easy does it, I have you," he said to her.

He carefully helped her back to an upright position then guided her to the chair next to his.

Rodney swam to the end of the pool and asked her if she was all right.

"Yes, I am just fine, thanks to this kind man."

"My name is Oliver Paden, at your service, madam," he said in his Irish brogue as he tipped his hat.

"Are you going to swim your laps now, Mom?" Rodney asked.

"In a little while, once I catch my breath," she replied.

"And you may as well sit right there while you recuperate," Mr. Paden said. "Would you like me to get you a drink?"

She blushed a moment, then said, "That would be nice. I would love a bottle of water."

When he left to get their drinks, Rodney thought she looked a bit confused, but happy.

He swam back to us, and we continued our game.

"Did I hear your mom say she was going to swim laps?" I asked Rodney.

"Yes, she is back to swimming laps for exercise, which she has done for years. It is helping her lose weight. As big as she is now, you should have seen her two months ago."

We all knew that her swimsuit was pink under her pink cover up, and the thought of her even bigger a few months ago was something we could not get out of our minds.

Soon Mom and Dad called us to go up, and all the other parents in our group followed suit.

As we all walked past Mr. Paden and Rodney's mom, she apologized for her rude behavior that morning at the beach. She told us she was very anxious about this first wedding she had designed flower girls' dresses for and that she was very sorry. She told us that she is very proud of what Rodney did, and she planned to speak to the lifeguard in the morning. She asked us to forgive her rudeness.

We said we understood and said that Rodney was a hero and that he would probably get some kind of badge as recognition.

Next Dad told her how watching Rodney do the CPR on the girl had taught us how to do it on the Skipper that afternoon. All were amazed to hear that story, and soon I was getting pats on the back as well.

Then we all headed up to our rooms, assuring her that we would talk more with her tomorrow.

Soon Rodney went to his room as well, leaving his mom talking with Mr. Paden.

As I was taking a shower, I was startled to see Paddy sitting on the soap dish. I am quite sure my feet came a good six inches off the shower floor when I saw him. Having somebody sitting on the soap dish while you are showering is quite a shock.

"'Tis nice to take a long hot shower to relax after such an excitin' day, right, laddie?"

"You can say that again."

"I'm in the mood for some of those yummy cupcakes that ye handed out at the pool tonight. Did ye save me one?"

"Paddy, I think you know very well that there was one left," I grinned and said.

"Sure and begorra, ye think that was just a coincidence?"

He laughed so hard, I thought the soap dish would fall off the wall.

"Okay, I will get it for you as soon as I get out of here. Hey, Paddy, did you plan to have Rodney's mom trip right there so Mr. Paden could save her? Cuz I think there is something very interesting about him, and I think you have some plan in mind."

"Yer very observant, lad. Always knew ye were as smart as a whip. Yes, I may have a trick or two up me sleeve. Rodney's ma is a good lady, with a heart of gold. She has had too much sadness in her life, and Lily and I are going to try to make her a wee bit happier."

"Where is Lily?" I asked, suddenly realizing I was naked.

"Ah, don't worry, laddie. Lily is much too much the lady to ever appear when she would embarrass somebody. She's a real classy gal."

Whew.

"Paddy, do you think Mr. Paden has a leprechaun, too?

It took a moment for him to answer.

"What I can tell ye, is this. Ye never know who has a leprechaun, and who doesn't. And ye can never ask another soul that question, as they wouldn't be able to answer ye anyway. 'Tis only for each lucky soul to keep his own leprechaun in his own heart, and only for his to trust in the same. Do ye understand, laddie?"

"Yes, I do. And Grampa told me I can never ask, or tell anybody about you, but I just get a feeling there is something special about him. I know he is very nice since he did not yell at me when I hit him in the head with the volleyball."

Paddy laughed and said that was almost as funny as me getting hit in the head with the volleyball.

I assumed he had a hand in that as well.

I got out of the shower and went to get the last cupcake for Paddy. I thought of the time Paddy ate pizza with Grampa and me just before the ski trip. Grampa had slipped him little pieces of pizza as Paddy sat beside him in the booth. And the waitress never even saw him.

I brought the cupcake back to the bathroom, where Paddy gleefully ate it on the counter.

The girls were knocking on the door, wanting to take their shower, so we just had a minute more.

"Tomorrow Sea Lady and I are going down to another sunken Spanish galleon ship. 'Tis a sight to behold, she tells me."

I was suddenly wishing I could go too, but I knew I had been given one magical trip, which is more than most people ever get. I wanted to ask if I could tag along, but somehow I knew not to ask.

"Thanks for me cake, laddie. Sure and begorra, 'tis late, and I need me beauty sleep, ye know."

With that, he wiped his little mouth on the corner of the napkin, took off his pointed green hat, bowed deeply, and was gone.

That night we sat on the balcony, as usual, eating our popcorn.

Rodney's mom was still down there sitting with Mr. Paden. We could hear them laughing, and then they walked down to the beach.

Chapter Twelve

The next morning was another beautiful, sunny day. I was anxious to get to the beach. The past few days had been the best of my life. All eight, almost nine, years of it.

Dad and I arrived at the pool just as Rodney was swimming laps.

"He is really a good swimmer," said Dad.

"He has been on a swim team for years, and then he also had a pool at his house. Can we get a pool, Dad?"

"Not any time soon, but maybe when Jennifer gets a little older."

We sat on the beach chairs, looking at the ocean, and I told Dad about Rodney and his mom. He told me that a lot of people gain a lot of weight, or lose their hair, or get really sad when they have so much sorrow. That is why you should never make fun of people, he said.

Mr. Paden came walking up the beach and sat beside us. He had a bag and had collected a lot of pretty shells and starfish.

Every time I spoke to him, I could swear I saw a twinkle in his eyes. He was just so cool.

The lifeguard was just getting set up, and Rodney joined us.

I asked Dad what we were going to do today, and he said that we were just going to hang out on the beach.

"Are you going to parasail?" Rodney asked.

"Can I, Dad?"

I had been watching them every day, but I assumed the answer would be no, especially from Mom, so I didn't bother.

"I will have to check and see the age limit, and then we can decide."

That sounded positive.

"I have scheduled ten o'clock to go," said Rodney. "Then Mom and I have to go to the wedding. She is both excited and sad about the twin flower girls."

"I hope it turns out good," I said.

I grabbed the boogie boards, and Dad, Rodney, Mr. Paden, and I went out to the water.

"I have never seen so many dolphins as I have this trip," said Mr. Paden.

I just nodded in agreement.

At ten on the dot, Rodney's mom came out to the beach, in her pink coverup, of course, and sat in a chair to watch him parasail. We all waved to him and watched as he sailed overhead.

What a glorious feeling, I thought. *What I wouldn't give to be able to fly.*

Mr. Paden had gone to sit beside Rodney's mom on another chair. They talked and laughed the whole time Rodney sailed overhead. He waved to us, and we could hear him laughing and yelling.

I couldn't wait to tell Grampa Mac all that had happened. I was glad to know I had this one person in the world that I could always talk to about Paddy O'Rourke.

By the time my mom got down to the beach, I had worked myself up to beg as much as was necessary to get her to let me parasail. Rodney was still talking about it, and I just had to do it. I knew that I would beg in a very undignified manner if necessary.

She finally got down to our beach chairs, cooler and all, and I began my pitch.

"Mom, I checked, and I am tall enough and old enough to parasail, and Rodney just did it and he is perfectly safe, so can I please do it too?"

"I knew you were going to ask to do that, and I have given it much thought. I have watched the guys running it, and I actually spoke to them already. There is a special harness they use for younger kids, and they do not go quite as high, so I think you may do it. Your dad and I have already decided."

What? That was too easy. Wow. Okay....

"Do you want to go now, or wait until all your friends get down here?"

"I will wait till they get here so they can watch, and then I bet their parents will let them do it, too."

Time dragged by, but soon they arrived, and the gang was together once again. We had one hour to kill before I made my first parasail trip.

We began talking, and as luck would have it, Kelly's condo was just below ours and Rob's was just below Bobby's. Once we figured that out, I got Jack and Bobby together and we decided to pull the spider trick on them. Aunt Nancy agreed to let us borrow it for that evening.

I could hardly wait, but soon it was time for my parasail flight.

I was harnessed in while all watched from the beach.

It was a wondrous thing, as I took off. The feeling of flying!

My stomach felt like it was a balloon floating up and down in my body.

As I reached the full height, I heard Paddy laughing beside me. I looked down, and he was sitting beside me, holding on to my harness strap. His little green hat was flattened out behind him because of the force of the wind, and I wondered how it even stayed on his head.

"Sure and begorra, laddie, 'tis a fine way to fly. Did I tell ye that we leprechauns love to para-hitch as well?"

"No, you left that one out, but you told me that you all ski-hitch, scuba-hitch, and sky-hitch with unsuspecting people, so this is not a surprise."

We looked down, and everybody waved as we flew over. Of course, they did not know that there were two of us up there. Paddy said he found the Spanish galleon shipwreck with Sea Lady and it had been amazing. He said it was sad to see it in such a deteriorated condition since she was such a beautiful ship when she set sail.

"What? You actually saw that ship sailing? When?"

"'Twas when she set sail from France. Me buddies and I had been there and stayed up on her sails and birdnest for most of the trip. We would come and go, and we enjoyed watching the poker games. The French and Spanish sailors did not like each other and got into lots of fistfights. Usually somebody ended up walking the plank. This particular ship got caught in a hurricane here in the Gulf and sank. If the crew had spent more time sailing and less time playing cards and fighting, they would have made it to New Orleans long before the hurricane hit and sank them."

I nodded, as if that was something to which I had given much thought.

Suddenly there was a snap, and we were caught up in a big gust of wind.

I heard screams from the beach below, and realized that the rope tying us to the boat had snapped and Paddy and I were quickly floating out to sea.

Paddy must have seen the look of panic cross my face because he was suddenly on my shoulder talking to me.

"No need to worry, laddie. We are going to be fine. Just a snafu in the boat line."

I saw that when the rope snapped, it got caught in the boat's motor, so he was unable to follow us as we headed out to sea.

"The boat driver has already spoken to the Coast Guard, and a helicopter and boat are on their way," Paddy said reassuringly."

"Are we going to crash into the ocean? With all the sharks?"

"No siree, ye have me word that ye will not crash. 'Tis going to be as smooth a landing as ye can imagine. Sea Lady is just below us, and she will keep any sharks away if we get so much as our toes wet."

I looked down, and there she was, jumping out of the water, as if she was calming my nerves.

We began slowing a bit and our altitude dropped. Soon we heard a helicopter, and Paddy sat down beside me so he would not be seen. The helicopter door was open, and a diver in a wetsuit was sitting there waving to me. He gave me the thumbs up, which relaxed me. The diver made a circular motion, meaning that they were going to follow behind me. I nodded that I understood, and the helicopter circled behind me. About ten minutes later, the helicopter came around in front of me again, and he pointed behind us, and I turned to look. There was a Coast Guard boat speeding toward us.

Unknown to me, the Coast Guard had already phoned the boat owner, and my family knew that I was in no danger of being lost and that they were following me. They were waiting for me to drop a little lower, and the plan was to grab the line and pull me in to the boat.

When I knew that I would not be lost at sea forever and that Paddy and Sea Lady were with me, I relaxed and actually enjoyed the feeling of freedom. A few sea gulls flew by, and except for the roar of the helicopter following me, it was very serene and peaceful.

"'Tis about time that I be heading off this ride laddie. Looks like yer rescue is about to happen, as we dropped a bit more. Don't worry. Trust me when I say that ye will have no harm come to ye from this rescue. Yer life is in good hands with the Coast Guard, and of course, Sea Lady and meself."

"I know that Paddy. I feel very safe. But I am glad that you were with me when this happened."

"Me too, laddie."

With that, he took off his hat, bowed, and was gone.

Soon the boat was below me, and one of the men on board yelled up with a bullhorn.

"Jason, are you okay?"

I nodded and gave him the thumbs up.

He smiled and told me that in a few more minutes, when the wind slowed and I dropped down just a bit more, their plan was to grab the rope hanging from my seat and pull me in. I nodded again and sat back to wait.

There was a tug, and suddenly their plan was in action. They had put my rope into a winch, and I was slowly being pulled down into the coolest boat I had ever seen.

Once on board, the captain introduced himself, and told me how brave I was. Then he took me on a tour of the boat and gave me some juice and cookies. He then asked me if I wanted to sit in his chair for the trip back to the beach. Of course I accepted his offer, and then he got my parents on the radio. When he heard my mom's voice, he handed me the mike, and I told her that I was safely in the boat and on my way back.

I could practically hear her fall into Dad's arms. I then spoke to Dad, and the girls. I told them to watch for our boat, and I whispered something to the captain. He nodded, and I told them I had a surprise for them and to get their cameras ready.

Soon the beach was in sight, and the boat came in as far as it could. As we approached, they saw me sitting in the captain's chair, with his hat on, blowing the horn.

I hope Mom gets lots of pictures, I thought to myself.

Then all the men on the boat shook my hand, and they launched a large raft with a motor, and I climbed down a ladder and got in.

Soon Mom and Dad and everybody else was hugging me and asking if I was scared to death.

"No, not really scared, more like excited. And anxious. Well, maybe a little scared, too."

"Well, I guess our parents will not let us parasail now," said Kelly.

"You got that right," his dad said.

That evening my parents agreed to take all five of us guys to dinner, and the girls stayed at the condo and ordered pizza with Jack's parents.

We went to the Pirate Ship restaurant, which was really cool. We ate outside by the gangplank, and the waiters were dressed like pirates.

Mom and Dad sat at their own table, and we sat by ourselves. We had a great time because the pirate waiters kept telling us scary stories about the gangplank and threatened to blindfold us and make us walk it if we did not eat our coleslaw.

Since I do not know a single kid who eats coleslaw, I felt our days were numbered. It was fun to participate in the game. We made all kinds of plans to overtake the pirate waiters, but they seemed to be one step ahead of us. We were not allowed to look over the side of the ship by the gangplank, but after dinner we were allowed to walk the gangplank one at a time. It was our punishment for not eating our coleslaw.

It was a cool set up since there was a trampoline under the gangplank, so we each got to jump off. Mom and Dad were waiting at the bottom for us.

Back at the hotel, Shannon and I ran up to Aunt Nancy's room to get the spider and fishing line.

Chapter Thirteen

That evening the teenagers were not playing volleyball, so my new gang, including Chloe, Mary, Bobby, Jack, Kelly, Patrick, and Rob, began playing. Mr. Paden had been watching us play, and when Rodney and his mom came down to the pool, we all stared in amazement. She had on a black swimsuit cover. Not pink.

Rodney joined our volleyball game, and his mom sat down beside Mr. Paden. We all whispered to Rodney to ask him where the pink went.

"It was the weirdest thing. After the wedding this afternoon, Mom told me that when she saw the twin flower girls walking down the aisle, she began crying. But it was a happy cry, not a sad cry. She had realized that Bridgette was in heaven and happy and that she wanted us to be happy, too."

"So she decided not to wear pink any more, in honor of Bridgette?"

"That's right. So we went shopping afterward and she bought all new clothes. Every color except pink."

"She looks so much happier now," said Chloe.

"She is. I see a big difference. And I think Mr. Paden has been talking to her a lot, so maybe he has helped."

Mr. Paden and Rodney's mom waved and yelled that they were going for a walk, and he put on his green hat.

"The therapist said that one day Mom would realize that the need to wear Bridgette's favorite color had gone away and that would be a healing day for us," said Rodney as he watched his mom walking away.

I am sure glad this is the day, I thought to myself.

We resumed our game, practicing our new tricks and the strategies we had been taught.

When the teenagers returned that night, they let us play with them for two games. After that we went to the pool, and after playing Marco Polo and Sharks and Minnows, we went upstairs to get a snack. We had not planned on leaving the condo that night because fireworks were scheduled. Mom bought stuff to grill on the large grill by the pool, and we ate on the balcony, watching the world below.

I saw Mr. Paden sitting on the beach by himself, and I asked Dad if I could go down and talk to him.

"Sure," said Dad. "But stay right there. No walking down by the fireworks set up."

"Don't worry, Dad. I learned my lesson last New Year's Eve when I botched the firecrackers and nearly lost my fingers. I want nothing to do with fireworks ever again."

"Good."

I walked down and sat by Mr. Paden. He had his hat on, and he took it off and put it on his lap.

"'Tis a fine evening, Jason."

"Yes, sir."

I did not know what to say. I just sat there looking at the ocean.

He must have sensed my loss of words and began asking me questions.

"Have you had an exciting spring break?"

I looked at him, and I could swear his eyes twinkled.

"You have no idea. This has been the trip of a lifetime."

"Ah, but at such a young age, laddie, 'tis me thought that ye will have many more special adventures."

Adventures, he said the word adventures. That is the word that Paddy had used.

I looked at him, and he winked at me.

Suddenly a Frisbee gently bumped into the back of his head. He bent over to pick it up as a little girl walked over to get it.

"Oh, I am so sorry," she said quietly.

"'Tis no problem, lassie," he said gently. "Me head is used to little bumps. 'Tis why I wear hats so much, to hide the bumps."

He smiled at her, and I saw the Frisbee. He turned it over, and tossed it to her. Nothing on it. No Notre Dame logo. Or anything else.

"Rodney's mom looked much happier today. I am glad she is not still wearing pink in honor of Bridgette any more," I said.

"Me too. 'Tis a breakthrough for her—and Rodney as well. I like her very much, and I hope she likes me."

"Where do you live, Jason?"

"In Atlanta, where all my friends are from. My grandparents live there, too."

I proceeded to tell him about Grampa Mac and how he always gets bumps on his head as well.

"It must be a family trait."

The fireworks were beginning, and soon everybody was beside us

We watched the fireworks, and even the girl Rodney had saved joined us. She seemed all back to normal, but she did not go in the ocean any more on this trip.

The next morning the lifeguard came and found us early and said that if we could find Rodney, he had an award for him. We all decided to make a ceremony out of it and got the girl he saved and her parents in on it as well. At ten A.M., We knocked on Rodney's door and told him that we were kidnapping him for a while. His mom had been notified by telephone and was in on the surprise. She had told Rodney to dress for brunch, and so he looked nice. He looked very confused, but they followed us..

Down at the pool, the fire marshall and lifeguard were there waiting for us. There was also a photographer, who was desperately trying to keep his camera dry. The girl Rodney saved, her parents and the hotel manager were there.

Mr. Paden stood beside Rodney's mom, who was wearing a dark green dress.

The fire marshall told everyone around the pool and beach area that we were all there to recognize the heroics of the junior lifeguard who saved this girl's life a few days earlier. Then the lifeguard put a medal tied with a ribbon around Rodney's neck and the photographer snapped the picture. "This will be published in your local hometown newspaper tomorrow," he told Rodney.

The hotel manager handed Rodney an envelope that included one week's free condo rental for his use whenever he wanted.

Rodney's mom was crying with happiness, and Mr. Paden took her hand.

Next the hotel manager motioned to the door and a large cart of muffins and juices and fruit was rolled out.

Needless to say, Rodney was overwhelmed and speechless. He had never been acknowledged for doing anything good, but he looked very pleased.

Suddenly there was a scream from the fifth floor balcony and we saw a woman flailing her arms madly at what we knew was a big furry, fake spider. The hotel manager took off running, and we saw the spider being quickly pulled up to the tenth floor balcony

The bratty cousins.

Aunt Nancy, who had been down at the pool with us, had not noticed the bratty cousins had sneaked up to their room.

In their haste to reel in the other secret spider that they bought and leave the condo before getting caught, Greg and David threw the pillows from their pillow fight moments earlier up off the floor, intending them to land on the sofa, out of their way. Instead the pillows hit the ceiling fan and chandelier over the dining room table, breaking both.

They ran out of the condo and into the elevator, intending to pretend they had been on another floor and therefore not capable of doing these dastardly deeds.

What a surprise for them when they stepped into the elevator to see the hotel manager and Aunt Nancy glaring at them.

Since this was not the first experience he had with these boys, he was not surprised to see them.

He grabbed each one by their collar and headed for their condo, whose door had been left open in their haste to leave. He surveyed the damage and stood there silently.

Aunt Nancy walked in behind him and was horrified. She told the manager that the condo would be cleaned immediately and that she would check out. He could keep the money she had already paid for the next two days to use for repairs. He nodded and said that would be satisfactory. She then told him that Greg and David would be paying for these repairs out of their own money and that she would let him know the rest of their punishment.

He shook his head, seemed to be sad for her having two such reckless boys, and left the room.

She ordered them to clean up and began packing up.

Then she knew what their punishment would be.

Like my mom, she believed that the punishment should fit the crime.

She went to the bedroom and called the manager. After explaining her plan, he laughed and agreed.

After they were all packed up, Aunt Nancy went down to the pool to tell us what had happened and that she was leaving to go back home.

I was not sad to hear that at all. It was all I could do to not jump up and down like a small kid.

She said she had to execute a plan first.

Aunt Nancy sat down with us, and suddenly the doors to the janitor's storage room opened. Out marched the manager, with Greg and David behind him. They were both wearing white jackets, like the groundskeepers wore. They pulled the maintenance cart behind them. Then they stopped, and each boy grabbed a broom and long-handled dustpan. They began sweeping up small bits of paper, cigarette butts, and gum wrappers around the pool and tennis courts. Then they each grabbed a trash bag and began picking up any trash along the hotel beach front and landscaped areas. The manager followed along behind them. They walked around the entire hotel grounds, picking up as they went.

I sat and watched, trying not to smile too much, as I knew they would try to get even with me later on at some point.

It was now quite late, and the manager finally let the boys put away the cart and hang up the white jackets. He then came over to Aunt Nancy and shook her hand. She told him they would be gone first thing in the morning and that the maids who would clean their condo would be quite happy to see how clean it would be. He smiled again and went back to his office.

We did not see Greg and David again this trip, and I was quite pleased to hear later that Aunt Nancy had the boys up half the night cleaning the condo, even scrubbing the showers and floor tiles. She even told my mom that she wished she had known that it was probably the boys who had damaged the other condo fire sprinklers and flooded the other condo, because she would have loved to have made them clean that mess up.

The next morning we decided that we better not do the hairy spider trick on Rob and Kelly. I surely did not want my little boy body wasting time picking up trash in front of everybody, even though their punishment was not for the trick but for the damage they had done to the condo.

As we sat on the balcony eating breakfast, we saw Rodney's mom walk out to the pool and dive in. She had on a dark blue swimsuit and she swam five laps. She was a very good swimmer, and I was thinking that she would probably lose a lot more weight soon and be able to swim fifty laps.

Mr. Paden came out as she was drying off, and they took a walk on the beach, hand in hand.

This was our last full day at the beach, and we spent it relaxing at the pool and beach. Rodney told us that he thought his mom and Mr. Paden would continue to see each other since he was retired and traveled a lot. He only lived one hundred miles from them, which was an easy drive.

"I am very happy for Mom, because this trip has been a breakthrough for her. She is finally beginning to smile and act like herself again," Rodney said.

"What is your mom's name?" I asked him.

"Brooke."

"Well, I think your mom and Oliver Paden will be very happy for many years," I said. "I have this feeling."

"Me too. And I am happy about it.

"And I am glad that you kept falling on me, because you really are a good kid," he told me.

"You are really cool, and thanks for not breaking my nose," I laughed.

That evening I went down to the beach and laid out my towel. The sand was still warm from the sun, and I closed my eyes. I had so much to tell Grampa Mac. I was remembering all that had happened on this spring break, and I could not wait until our next vacation. I wondered where we would go and what adventure awaited me.